TRANSFORMERS
REVENGE OF THE FALLEN

I Am Optimus Prime

Adapted by Jennifer Frantz
Illustrations by Guido Guidi
Based on the Screenplay by
Ehren Kruger & Alex Kurtzman & Roberto Orci

Optimus Prime is the brave leader
of the Autobots.
They are robots in disguise!

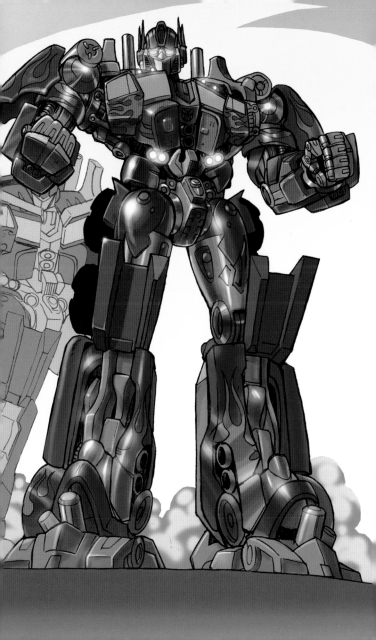

Optimus is not just any 'bot.

He is the last of the great Primes,

a line of noble robots.

They come from

the planet Cybertron.

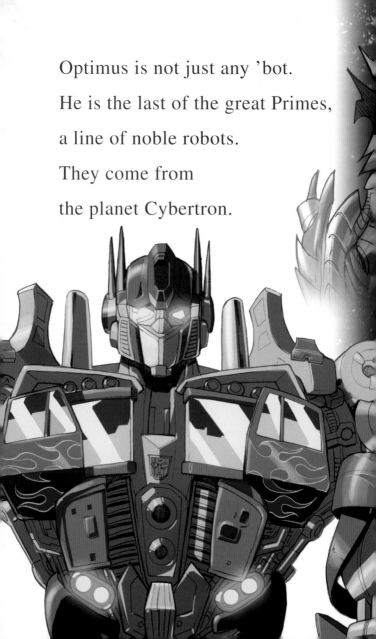

Like all true Primes,

Optimus fights for what is right.

Here on planet Earth,

Optimus Prime

is a friend to humans.

Side by side,

humans and Autobots battled Megatron

and his evil Decepticons.

Now Earth has a new threat.

And Optimus Prime has a new enemy.

The enemy's name is The Fallen.

The Fallen is even more evil
and powerful than Megatron.
He feeds on energy,
growing stronger and stronger.
The Fallen wants to absorb
the sun's energy
and destroy planet Earth.

Optimus Prime must
stop The Fallen.
But he is not alone!

The brave Autobots are ready to do whatever their leader asks.

Look out, Decepticons!
The Twins might look little
but they are double trouble.

Ironhide and Optimus Prime
make a great team.
Together they defeat the evil Demolisher.

Bumblebee is a loyal 'bot.

He will go anywhere

to help a friend.

Sideswipe is a fearless fighter.

He will do anything

for Optimus Prime.

The battle is on!
The Autobots face off
against the Decepticons.

Optimus Prime is ready to rumble!

Bumblebee blasts
a bulldozing Decepticon!
Bumblebee is small and fast.

Bumblebee has never fought better.

He wins this battle!

The Twins take on
the deadly Devastator.

This giant 'bot
is bad news!

In the end,

Optimus Prime sends The Fallen

screaming into space.

The sun is saved.

Optimus made the Earth safe
from Decepticons.
At least, for now.